THE TERRIBLE
CHENOO

D1632626

For Matthew –
maybe monsters can
mellow! – F. P.

To my dear
nephew Joachim
– S. F.

Barefoot Books
2067 Massachusetts Ave
Cambridge, MA 02140

Barefoot Books
29/30 Fitzroy Square
London, W1T 6LQ

Series Editor: Gina Nuttall

Text copyright © 2003 by Fran Parnell. Illustrations copyright © 2003 & 2011 by Sophie Fatus
The moral rights of Fran Parnell and Sophie Fatus have been asserted

First published in the United States of America by Barefoot Books, Inc
and in Great Britain by Barefoot Books, Ltd in 2011
This paperback edition first published in 2020
This story is an abridged version of a chapter of
The Barefoot Book of Monsters, published in 2003. All rights reserved

Graphic design by Helen Chapman, West Yorkshire, UK
Reproduction by B&P International, Hong Kong.
Printed in China on 100% acid-free paper by Printplus, Ltd
This book was typeset in Carrotcake, Sassoon Primary and Mr Anteater
The illustrations were prepared in acrylics

Sources:
Leland, Charles G. The Algonquin Legends of New England.
Houghton Mifflin Company, Boston, 1884.

Spence, Lewis. Myths and Legends of the North American Indian.
George G. Harrap & Co., London, 1914.

Thompson, Stith. Tales of the Northern American Indians.
Harvard University Press, Cambridge, Massachusetts, 1929.

ISBN 978-1-78285-844-7

British Cataloguing-in-Publication Data: a catalogue
record for this book is available from the British Library

Library of Congress Cataloging-in-Publication Data
is available under LCCN 2011002937

1 3 5 7 9 8 6 4 2

THE TERRIBLE CHENOO

A Tale from Algonquian Nations

Retold by Fran Parnell

Illustrated by Sophie Fatus

Barefoot Books

step inside a story

CONTENTS

CHAPTER 1

Noises in the Bushes

Long, long ago in an Algonquian nation, there lived a man and his wife. One autumn, they decided to go on a hunting trip. They left their tribe and journeyed far away to the northwest.

When they found a clearing in the
pine forest, they set up their tepee.
"We will stay here for the winter," the
man and his wife agreed.

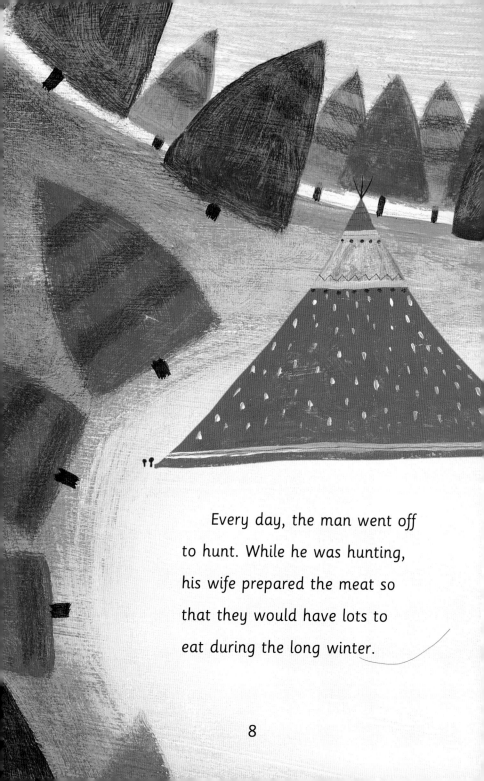

Every day, the man went off to hunt. While he was hunting, his wife prepared the meat so that they would have lots to eat during the long winter.

8

Happy hunting!

All went well for a time.
The weather was fine and
there were plenty of wild
animals to hunt. The husband
and wife were happy.

One breezy day, while the man
was hunting, the woman went to
gather more wood for the fire.

Suddenly, there was a
WHOOSH!

The woman heard a sharp
whistle of wind. She felt an icy gust
on her face. There was a strange
rustling noise in the bushes nearby.
The woman looked up and what
she saw was . . . terrible!

11

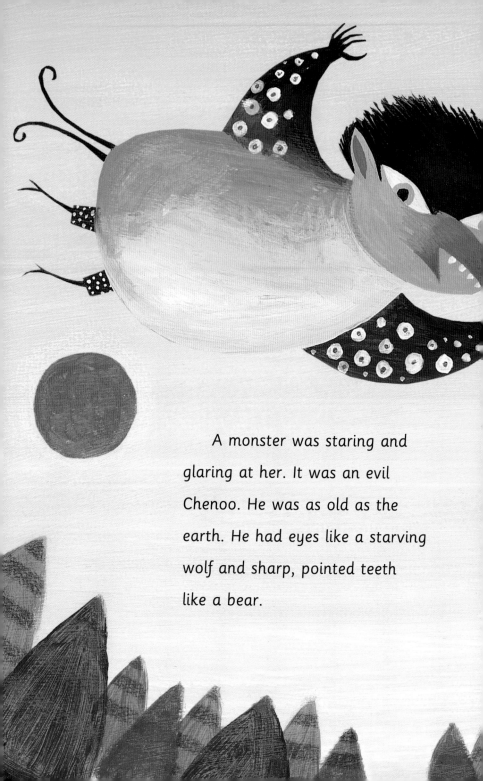

A monster was staring and
glaring at her. It was an evil
Chenoo. He was as old as the
earth. He had eyes like a starving
wolf and sharp, pointed teeth
like a bear.

His cruel heart was colder than ice. It thumped in his chest like a booming drum. The Chenoo had journeyed from the far, far north. He had flown on the frosty wind and the long flight had made him hungry — very, VERY hungry.

In fact, he was STARVING!
What he wanted was a bite of
nice, juicy meat.

The woman trembled all over
with fear.

CHAPTER 2

The Woman's Clever Plan

What shall I do?

The woman was very afraid, but she was also very clever. She was as clever as a fox. She did not want to be the Chenoo's next meal, so she thought of a plan.

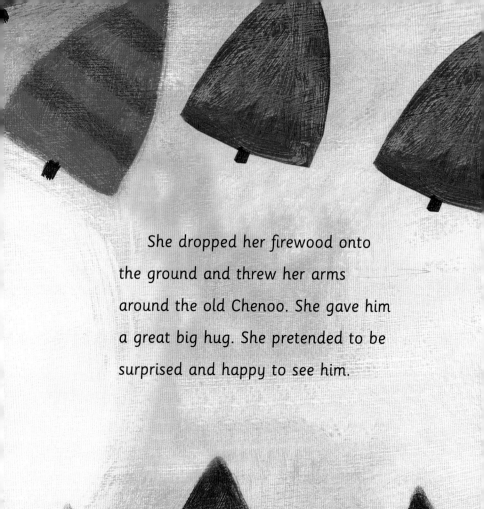

She dropped her firewood onto
the ground and threw her arms
around the old Chenoo. She gave him
a great big hug. She pretended to be
surprised and happy to see him.

"Father!" she cried. "What a
wonderful surprise! How well you
look! And how good of you to travel
all this way to visit us!"

Then she took a step backwards
and looked him up and down. A
puzzled look crossed her face.

"But what has happened to
your clothes, Father? You must
be frozen through! Come into the
tepee and warm yourself up." And,
chattering away, she took the
monster's hand and led him out
of the bushes.

The Chenoo was very surprised.
He had eaten plenty of people
before. Usually they screamed or
tried to run off or fainted before he
gobbled them up. But this woman
did none of those things.

That's better.

The Chenoo was so surprised that he forgot all about eating the woman. He followed her like a child into the tepee. Then he let her dress him in a deerskin shirt, leather trousers and a fine pair of moccasins. Soon he was wrapped up as snugly as a baby in a papoose.

"There now, Father. Isn't that better?" asked the woman.

"I'll just go and collect some sticks to build up the fire. With a good bright blaze, your old bones will be warm again in no time."

The woman scurried out of the tepee,
but soon her knees were trembling again
because the terrible Chenoo picked up an
axe and followed her outside.

"Oh dear!" the woman exclaimed.

"He is going to chop me up!"

CHAPTER 3

Stop Chopping, Chenoo!

The Chenoo held the axe and followed the woman outside. But he did not chop her up. Instead, he began to chop down the tall forest trees.

He chopped and he chopped. The huge pine trees toppled easily around him. It was as if he was just cutting down blades of grass.

The woman watched in wonder. Soon
the Chenoo had chopped down half the
forest. Finally, the woman shouted, "Enough,
Father! We have enough wood now!"

Stop!

The Chenoo stopped chopping. He did not say a word. He began to pick up the fallen trees and pile them neatly behind the tepee.

Just then, the woman saw her husband coming. He was walking in and out of the trunks of the fallen trees.

He looked around in amazement.
Quickly, the woman went over to him.
She wanted to talk to him before the
monster saw him.

She told her husband what had
happened. So, when the husband
walked up to the Chenoo, he knew
just what to say.

CHAPTER 4

Something Strange Happens

Hello!

"Father-in-law!" he cried. "How kind of you to travel all this way to see us! I have caught enough food today for all of us. We can have a splendid meal while you tell us the news from home!"

The Chenoo stayed silent
when they all sat down to eat.
The husband and his wife were
still terrified of the monster, but
they ate well. While they ate,
they chatted about their tribe.

They gossiped about this and that. They wondered what their family and friends were doing. Were they all safe and well?

The man and his wife offered the
monster fresh meat, dried pumpkin
and hot corn coffee, but the Chenoo
did not eat.

They are
so nice.

He just listened to their talk.
Slowly a gentle look appeared on his
terrible face.

Screech! Screech!

He had never had a family or any friends. Chenoos attacked each other whenever they met. They would scream and screech angrily. Their bodies would grow huge until their heads touched the clouds. They would fight for days and days.

The sky thundered and the earth shook with their screams. The noise was so terrible that you could hear it a thousand miles away. The people in the south would lie awake at night with their teeth chattering, listening to the terrible noise.

The winner of the Chenoo battle
would leap onto one of the strong
winds that blew through the land. He
would fly off to find another monster to
fight or a trembling human to eat.

But something very strange happened to this Chenoo as he listened to the man and the woman. They had welcomed the Chenoo into their home. They had given him clothes and offered him food.

His heart danced for joy when they spoke to him gently and called him "Father." He could not believe it. The monster's icy heart was warmed by their kindness.

All his cruel and violent thoughts
disappeared. He stopped wanting
to eat people. There and then he
decided that he wanted to stay with
them for the rest of his life.

CHAPTER 5

Friends Forever

The Chenoo lived with the man and woman from then on. They were surprised, but soon they were no longer afraid of the monster. In fact, he no longer seemed to be a monster to them.

He was very friendly and helpful. He helped the man to hunt wild animals and he helped the woman to chop firewood.

Soon winter came. The snow was too
deep to hunt. So the Chenoo helped the
man to make new arrows. He also helped
the woman to make new clothes. The
woman and the Chenoo sewed beads and
porcupine quills onto the clothes.

In the long winter evenings,
they all huddled by the fire under
thick blankets. The Chenoo made up
magical stories and told them to the
man and his wife.

The man and woman began to
love the old Chenoo. The Chenoo was
like a true member of their family.

When spring came again, the snow on
the pine trees melted and the river thawed.
The man and the woman prepared to
return to their tribe.

The Chenoo went with them. He
carried the tepee on his back and walked
along with huge monster steps.

As they went further and further south, the Chenoo's steps got shorter and shorter. He became weaker and weaker. The warm spring air in the south took his strength away.

The woman and the man begged him to return to his home. However, the Chenoo had changed too much to go back. Besides, he had promised to stay with the man and woman forever.

So he walked on. As they got closer to the man and woman's tribe, the Chenoo was too tired and too weak to walk. So the man and the woman carried the old Chenoo between them.

I am so tired!

When they reached the tribe, all the people gathered around the monster in wonder. His face had once been terrible to look at. Now it was peaceful. So the people were not afraid of him. In fact, everyone did their best to help the Chenoo.

But he was old and tired and the warm southern air was wearing him away. At last, his frozen heart thawed out completely. The Chenoo died — but he died the happiest Chenoo in the land.

He had found something that no other Chenoo had found before. He had found true friendship.